C000116826

In My Own Write
A Pot-Pourri of Literary Endeavour

Andrew G. Lockhart

Magda Green Books

Published in the United Kingdom by Magda Green Books,
Northamptonshire

ISBN: 979 8 65223 190 3

Other publications by the same author:

NOVELS
The Il-khan's Wife (e-book)
The Tiger and the Cauldron (e-book)
The Dark Side of the Fylfot (e-book)
Sweeter Than Wine (e-book and paperback)
(*as Drew Greenfield*)
Dark Inheritance (e-book)
NON-FICTION
The Lion, the Sun and the Eternal Blue Sky (e-book)
It's a Fantasy World! (e-book and paperback)
Classic Reviews (e-book and paperback)
Tapestry (e-book and hardback*)
Patterns (hardback only*)
* *limited editions family history*

In My Own Write

CONTENTS

In My Own Write

Introduction – an apology

This short miscellany has no single theme. It is a *pot-pourri* of my shorter jottings of the past twenty-five years, put together in no particular order with the sole purpose of amusing and entertaining the reader. A few of the pieces have been published before, others were written for friends and others still have never seen the light of day – and probably ought not to see it now. But *hey* . . . writers are an odd bunch. Sometimes we can't resist digging around in the attic.

Which reminds me: there are personal stories behind some of the pieces. *Leaving South Africa* is a reimagining of my mother's experience on leaving her first home about a century ago. *Christmas with Mr Selfridge* was a themed Christmas story for *Creative Minds*, my local writers' group. *Feneticks Bee Dammd* and *A Bat's Ear View* were written while I was a member of a choir, and inspired by experiences during that period of my life. *Mountain and Flood* recalls childhood holidays. *Travelling Companions* is the oldest offering, a short story written in the nineties when I was toying with ideas for a *scifi* novel.

Apart from some minor editing of spelling, grammar and out-of-date references, all the stories, poems and articles here are as I originally wrote them (warts and all). But if by chance there's something to your taste, reviews are always welcome.

Andrew G. Lockhart
June 2020

In My Own Write

Stories

In My Own Write

The Attic

A whiff of something unexplained, alien, reaches me through the half-open trapdoor. I fumble for the light switch just inside on the floor, find it and flip it on. Nothing happens. The bulb has gone. Something crawls across my hand and I draw it back instinctively. The ladder creaks and wobbles underneath my feet.

Just a spider. The attic is probably full of them. I heave upwards, slide the trapdoor back and thrust my head and shoulders into the attic space. A blast of icy air meets my face. The skylight window, encrusted with God-knows how many years of dust and grime, has cracked and a triangle of glass is missing.

I cough on the dust and damp. How long has it been like this, I wonder. Thirty-five years have gone by since my sister and I played in this room. My memories, cloudy now, are of freshly-emulsioned walls and the smell of pine disinfectant. I remember the sound of hammering – and the occasional expletive echoing round the roof space – as my father worked on the flooring and the insulation. The cross-beams were too low to accommodate a fully-grown man. Moreover, wearing safety goggles instead of his customary spectacles, he was dangerously short-sighted. My mother too, before arthritis claimed her hips and knees, would scamper up the pull-down ladder we had then to clean and vacuum for us. She could work standing with an inch or two to spare.

I grip the frame of the trapdoor, allow it to take my weight, and lever myself over the edge. The old wooden ladder, borrowed from a neighbour, stops short of the gap by a good three feet. No pull-down now. The fastenings had loosened and my father had deemed it unsafe.

On the window side, there is just enough light for me to see the hazards – a missing floorboard, a brick, splinters of glass everywhere. Crouching, I brush the strands of cobweb from the nearest rafters and stand up between them. A soggy heap of moss, grit and leaves has collected under the broken pane. The insulating panels that form the makeshift walls bulge and run with green slime. I smell the decay. The remaining pieces of furniture, my school desk minus lid, a wicker chair and our old holiday trunk are thick with decades of dust.

A sports car screams past in the street outside, the Doppler effect intensified by the hollow stillness of my surroundings. Why did I come, I ask myself? The house has too many ghosts: grandparents and parents have gone, and now my sister ... I suppose I want to see where it happened, want to have a last look at the old place, my inheritance, before I sell.

The alien smell is stronger now but I cannot locate the source. Then I see them, grotesque shapes, shadows thrown by the failing daylight in the far corner. Hanging, dead or alive I cannot tell, from one of the crossbeams. I cough again, reacting to both dust and stench. There is a flutter of wings and one skims past my nose. Another narrowly avoids my hair, panicking, squeaking.

Protected, claiming territory that was once mine.

ΩΩΩ

The Snakes of Horus

'We're safe for now. They can't get in.'

I risked a glance at Jude out of the corner of my eye. I couldn't, I daren't allow my attention to be diverted from the window. She was statuesque, her face drawn in a rigid mask, her eyes staring, her arms crossed and her hands tightly gripping her shoulders. Somehow she had lost a glove and her knuckles were bruised and red.

'And we can't get out! We can't take off!' She laughed hysterically. Then the sharp intake and rapid exhalation of her breathing were the only sounds I could hear in the dimly-lit module. Jude was a brilliant theorist, but she was a lab scientist, a computer kid. She was of no use in a crisis.

'We have to concentrate on fixing the engine,' I snapped. 'Kathy?'

'Working on it!'

'Ben . . .' Jude was moaning now, her body shaken by gigantic sobs. 'Snakes . . . We have to do something.'

'He's beyond help now,' I said with as much sympathy as I could muster; there was no time for it. They had been an item, Jude and Ben, since we began training for the expedition three years ago. 'We can do our mourning later.'

I had no confidence in the plate glass of the window. Two inches thick and built to contain our atmosphere, it was still vulnerable to attack from outside. We had all seen the creatures in action and knew what they were capable of. Those enormous jowls with their hideous serrated teeth could snap a man or woman in half. I had watched them, sick to my stomach and retching, as they opened and closed again over the mangled remains of one of the team. *Gerard, our biochemist, thirty years old with a wife and kids back on Earth.*

I had gasped in horror as the swinging tail of a female snake caught Ben, our navigator, off balance, felling him to the alien dust and shattering his helmet. Jude had calculated that we could survive eight minutes in the Horus atmosphere, but it hadn't been proved and never would be now. Ben had lasted barely ten seconds before the creature sank her teeth in his arm and struck him with her poisonous tail. I had heard the snapping of his bones and the creaking of his skin as he changed, growing before my eyes into one of the monstrosities that now paraded hungrily outside in the blue, moonlit terrain.

I'd hesitated no more than a second before running. Jude had stopped to help her boyfriend but it was too late. Kathy pulled her away. There was nothing any of us could do. The three of us, Jude, Kathy and I had only just made it back inside.

The first inhabited exoplanet and its dominant life-form were deadly serpents!

The window shuddered as the head of the alpha male, by far the largest of the creatures, thudded against it. The glass held. Jude screamed.

'It'll be OK.' I tried to reassure her but feeling all the while that our situation was hopeless. Kathy was working frantically at the engine, trying to start it again, but in the minutes since we slammed the module door on the monster snakes, it'd done no more than stutter and die. And that was what the three of us who were left would do if she didn't fix it soon.

There were four monster snakes now, the original three and the one that had once been Ben. We still couldn't be sure what he had become – male or female. It really didn't matter. Only the alpha was carnivorous but the females carried the virus that apparently destroyed human DNA and replaced it with their own. Going outside in our suits to collect soil and rock samples hadn't been the smartest thing we'd done. Unless Kathy could restart that engine soon and take us into orbit and back to the ship, we were done for.

The alpha's head connected with the window – twice. The glass shuddered again, the module door too as an armoured tail crashed against the steel. The choice was not one I wanted to make: slow death by poisoned air; swallowed whole, turned into a shapeless mass of blood, flesh and bone in the alpha's intestine; or become one of the creatures myself.

We had no weapons capable of defeating them. Guns were useless. Gerard and Ben had tried. The seconds taken to shoot had cost them their lives. Even if we had a knife or sword sharp enough to pierce their scaly hides, how could any of us get close enough? How could we avoid those sharp, tissue-tearing fangs or those scything tails with their deadly sting?

Outside, the landscape was darkening. The three blue moons of Horus were sinking to the horizon. The largest, so clear that I could see clouds moving across its surface, was already only a half disc at the edge of the desert. Any hope that the snakes would dislike the darkness was fading. If anything, the night seemed to vitalise their efforts to reach us.

'Help me here,' Kathy yelled and I backed up, still keeping my eye on the window. Jude was a helpless, cringing wreck in the pilot's seat. 'I'm going to count to five then I want you to kick that lever. Hard!'

She pulled a switch and fiddled with an electro-spanner at the back of the motor casing. ' . . . four, five . . . *now!*'

I struck the lever as hard as I could with my right foot. The motor growled but didn't start.

The window shuddered once more as the alpha creature butted it with his head, its jaws wide, its dripping tongue drawing a band of bloody slime across the pane. I saw its eyes, pale green and frighteningly intelligent, peer into the glass. *Hesitating between brute strength and strategy.* It knew we were running out of oxygen. I could almost read its mind; it wouldn't give up. *Better to wait?*

'Fuck! *Again,*' screeched Kathy. She pulled the switch again and I kicked with all the strength I could muster. An excruciating pain shot up my leg and I guessed my foot was broken.

The motor stuttered twice, coughed and roared into life. Kathy gave a triumphant whoop. Jude still seemed paralysed with terror

'Ten seconds more and you take it,' Kathy said to me.

I bundled Jude into a passenger seat and settled myself into the pilot's chair. Kathy took her position next to me. The engine noise became an expectant and familiar whine as I eased the module into the air. The large moon had almost set but there were two others. One gibbous, one full. I could still see the huge snakes writhing below and snapping at our vapour trail. Time slowed as we gained height. The seconds seemed like minutes. With all my concentration on the controls, there was no time for conversation. If only the repair held until we reached escape velocity.

The module soared into the upper atmosphere. The snakes of Horus were tiny fading specks on the moonlit desert. In a few moments we would make ship orbit. I sighed with relief and turned to grin at my two companions.

'We made it!'

Kathy stared back at me. Her expression was one of abject terror.

'Look at Jude,' she hissed.

I looked but there was really no need. I heard the sound of ripping nylon, the scrunch of pulverising skeleton, the creak of sinew and muscle that already was no longer human. None of us had been stung; that I knew with certainty. But we had no way of knowing the snakes had other, slower means of infecting us, of transferring their genes. A cold tremor of fear crawled along my spine. I remembered Jude's bruised, swollen hand. She had touched Ben. She must have; the venom was in her system.

We would not make it back safely. None of us would ever see Earth again.

Jude was already changing.

ΩΩΩ

Farewell to South Africa

The taxi pulled up on the quayside. From my seat in the back, I looked up at the massive hull of the ship in the berth.

Now that the time had come, I didn't want to go. I didn't want to leave South Africa, the only home I had ever known. I missed the mission school and my friends, and I did not want to trade them for a new life with people and places I didn't know. Worst of all, I still missed my father, now dead seven years. I was afraid of leaving him behind, of forgetting him and the memories of the short years we had shared.

The driver left the motor running as he helped us alight. He unloaded our hand luggage. We had sent on our trunks and they would already be delivered to our cabin.

My mother paid the driver and added a small tip. Now that the main breadwinner was gone, we weren't rich, but there was such a thing as pride.

'It'll be all right, Annie,' my mother said, picking up her bag and hugging my shoulders with her free hand. She seemed to understand what I was feeling but somehow it didn't help. I began to cry and buried my face in the folds of her cape.

It would be my fifth crossing. However, this trip would be different. My mother had made it clear that we would be spending more than just a few weeks in Scotland, the country she had left fifteen years earlier to marry my father in Boksburg. She hadn't really explained why she wanted to leave Africa or how long she expected us to be away. She had even talked about sending me to school in Britain.

That made things worse. I could conceive of no reasons that made sense why we would leave our comfortable, warm lives for faraway Scotland. I had been there and hadn't liked it much. The weather was cold and dull and the people spoke with a funny accent, all *ayes* and *ocks* and long, rumbling *rrr*s. My grandpa had become quite angry when I said I didn't understand him. My uncles had smelled of tobacco smoke.

For a few moments, I enjoyed the comfort of my mother's embrace. Then I withdrew from her bosom, sniffed and wiped my damp face on the sleeve of my new travelling frock.

'Use a handkerchief, Annie,' my mother chided. 'Remember you're a young lady!'

Two officials of the mail-ship company were waiting to inspect our tickets and our papers. My mother handed them over and we waited. The procedure seemed to take forever. I passed the time staring at other passengers who had passed through and were making their way up the gangplank - stiff and sullen strangers I had no intention of befriending.

Our embarkation approved, my mother squeezed my shoulder again and kissed me gently on the forehead.

'It'll be all right, Annie. It really will. We have one another and that's all that matters, isn't it?'

ΩΩΩ

Christmas with Mr Selfridge

In 1918, nine years after opening his famous London Oxford Street department store, Harry Gordon Selfridge commissioned an architect to design a spectacular tower to sit on top of the building. The tower was never built but ....

'I don't want to, Jake!'

Kylie's lower lip trembled as she looked up her brother. Standing on the bottom step, he seemed so much taller though they were nearly the same height. Jake was eight, only a year and a half older. There had been a chain across the passageway with a notice dangling from it. Kylie couldn't read the long words, but Jake had ducked under anyway.

'I want to go back,' she said. 'Mummy said to wait in the toy department.'

'Come on,' he urged. 'It'll be fun. I want to see what's at the top.'

'It's creepy. There aren't any lights. Santa Claus can't have gone this way.'

'He must have, Kylie. There aren't any other doors. Just these stairs.'

'I don't think we're supposed to be here,' Kylie said.

Jake made a face. He gave a gesture of impatience before hopping onto the next step. 'You wanted to see Father Christmas. Well, now's your chance.'

Kylie pouted. 'That wasn't really Santa. He's just an old man dressed up in a red suit and a beard. For the babies!'

'Well, I'm going up.'

'No, Jake!'

'Scaredy-cat! Kylie scaredy-cat!'

'Am not!'

'Are so!'

'Daddy said Sell *Fridges* was haunted.'

'It's *Self* Ridges,' Jake said. He adopted his most know-all, adult stance. 'Anyhow, there are no such things as ghosts.' He stepped down to the bottom tread and held out a podgy hand.

'O.K.' She hesitated, then gripped his fingers tightly and followed him as he took to the staircase. It curved to the right and into a helix before disappearing into the well of the tower.

There was just enough width to allow them to go abreast. It wasn't exactly bright but there was enough daylight filtering in to enable them to see the way ahead. They climbed together, hand in hand. Kylie counted the steps. She reached fifty-nine and stopped. 'I don't know sixties and seventies,' she breathed.

'They're the same as forties and fifties, silly,' said Jake. 'Sixty-one, sixty-two ... Anyway, it can't be far now.'

'I want to go back. Mummy will be worried.'

'Don't be such a baby, Kylie. Come on!' He counted another thirty steps for her and to Kylie's surprise the staircase came to an end in a broad platform. They were in a sort of room with big windows and a square-patterned carpet. The man from the toy department was sitting at a big desk in the middle. He still had on the Father Christmas outfit but had pulled the beard down over his chin so that he looked as if he were wearing a fluffy white scarf. He had put on gold-rimmed spectacles and was studying some papers in front of him.

'I told you.' Kylie let go of Jake's hand and just stared. 'He's not Father Christmas!'

The man looked up. He hastily replaced the beard but not before Kylie noticed he had a big black moustache that curled up at the ends. 'So who have we here?' he enquired.

'I'm Jake,' said Jake, stepping forward boldly. 'Jake Spenser. This is my sister Kylie. She's only six. She wanted to see Father Christmas.'

The man coughed but Kylie didn't think his face unkind or his manner unfriendly. 'How did you get in here? Are you lost?'

'We followed you from the toy shop,' Jake said.

'And I suppose a chain across the entrance with a notice "*Private - Management Only*" isn't enough of a deterrent.' He paused and laughed heartily. It was a very Father-Christmassy laugh. 'What am I saying? You probably don't know the meaning of the word management - or deterrent. Where are your mummy and daddy?'

'There's just Mummy. She's buying some Christmas presents.' Kylie was over her surprise and found her voice. 'You're not really Santa Claus, are you?'

'No, I'm Harry Gordon Selfridge.'

'Oh,' said Jake. 'It's your shop. *Self* Ridges.'

'Sell *Fridges*,' Kylie repeated, but with the changed emphasis. She giggled.

The man laughed again. 'We don't only sell fridges, young lady, as you know. And where I come from we call them ice boxes. Now, I think I'm going to have to take you to find your mother.'

'Why do you call them ice boxes?' Kylie asked.

'Well, I guess that's because I'm an American,' said Mr Selfridge. 'That's what Americans do. And they keep things cold, don't they? Like ice.' He rose from his chair. 'I tell you what, Kylie and Jake, would you like to see what London looks like from up here before we go?'

'Yes please, sir,' said Jake.

'Yes please, Mr Sell *Fridges*,' said Kylie.

Mr Selfridge went towards one of the windows and the children followed.

Kylie felt herself hoisted in the air and a moment later she was perched on Mr Selfridge's shoulder peering down on an Oxford Street bustling with Christmas shoppers. There was a policeman on a horse, two buses and some other traffic. The people were the size of insects and the cars looked very strange indeed. She glanced across at Jake, sitting on the shop owner's other shoulder. 'Doesn't everything look funny from up here?' she said. 'It's like being in an aeroplane.'

'Have you been in an aeroplane, Kylie?' Mr Selfridge asked.

'Course. Haven't you?'

'Sure. Twice, as a matter of fact. Now, I think we'd better go down to the store. Instead of the stairs, we'll take the quick route.' He gestured to a glass door on the other side of the room before crouching to let them jump down from his shoulders.

Mr Selfridge, still wearing his beard, slid the door to one side revealing a tiny elevator. There were only two buttons and he pressed the lower one marked *S*.

Kylie had been in an elevator several times and expected a shudder as they started to move, and when they stopped. This time she felt no sensation at all other than a feeling of great excitement. Christmas was only a week away.

The lift door opened. Mrs Spenser was carrying a big square parcel under one arm and in her other hand two carrier bags.

'Mummy!' Kylie rushed forward to hug her mother around the waist. Jake followed more sedately.

Mrs Spenser ruffled his hair. 'There you both are! I thought I'd lost you.'

'We've had a lovely time, Mummy.' Kylie tried unsuccessfully to peer into one of the carrier bags. 'We've been up in the tower. We went to see Father Christmas and we looked down on Oxford Street but everything looked so funny.'

'What do you mean, up in the tower? What tower? Jake, what have you been telling your sister?'

'We climbed the stairs,' Jake said. 'Then Mr Selfridge brought us down in his lift.' He turned round to look for the store owner.

Kylie turned too and stared, her eyes wide and her mouth gaping. What a moment ago had been a transparent lift door was now a much more solid one of wood. The sign above it read *Toilets*.

The man in the Father Christmas costume was nowhere to be seen.

ΩΩΩ

Travelling Companions

'Kris-mus?' The music salesman savoured the sound, dwelling on the second syllable. 'K-R-I-S-M-U-S?' he spelled.

'No, K-R-I-S-M-A-S,' corrected the slender blonde woman who was his sole travelling companion in the first-class compartment of the space shuttle.

'Really?' The salesman looked at her approvingly. She was beautiful, he thought, but somehow inviolable. Young, yet ageless. He had an eye for beautiful women, or so he imagined.

'Yes. The last syllable means a festival or a celebration in Old Terran.'

It was strange he had not noticed her at the station. Nor had he seen her come on board. He became aware of her only when she took the seat opposite and addressed him. Now, he was conscious of nothing else but her beauty and the soft sensuous tone of her voice. Other than that, there was only the outer silence of space.

As he waited for her to continue, the salesman studied her finely-sculpted features. Her high cheekbones had little colour and no make-up, and her delicate mouth was untouched by lipstick. He wondered if she would respond to a compliment about her appearance, or whether she would prefer a more subtle approach.

He was going to Terra, he had told her in response to her enquiry. 'For Krismas?' she had asked in surprise. He had not understood the word.

'It's an ancient festival,' she explained. 'Prehistoric in fact. The Terrans celebrated it in the days before space flight. It always takes place at the winter solstice of the northern hemisphere. Summer at the south. There is singing and dancing, and the people exchange gifts.'

The salesman knitted his brows. He rubbed his nose with his finger. What in the Cosmos was singing?

The woman laughed at his discomposure.

'Singing is music produced by the human voice,' she explained. 'It was once widespread in the Galaxy, but is now rather rare. Apart from Terra . . .'

'You are very knowledgeable,' interrupted the salesman. 'How is it I've never heard all that?'

His companion smiled sadly.

'Education in the outer planets is not what it was,' she said. 'But I used to live there. On Terra, I mean. A long time ago.'

It cannot have been so very long ago, the salesman thought. The cabin had been dimmed for the space warp but he could see her clearly enough. He put her age at 30, just a couple of years older than himself.

'Do you mind if I ask your name?' he asked.

'Not at all. It's Cecile.'

'Mine's Madeas.'

'Yes, I know.'

Madeas leant forward is his seat and looked at her strangely. How could she know that, he wondered. And it was odd how, at that moment, the dimmed lights began to play tricks with his eyes. Cecile's face seemed momentarily to shimmer and fade.

'How?'

'It was visible in the identity panel of your suitcase. The one you put in the cabin locker. You must have forgotten to encode it. *Madeas Ozarr*,' she quoted. '*Citizen of Galiteria; age 28; profession music salesman.* You are a musician?'

Her face showed unusual interest. Everything

about her was unusual, thought Madeas. She had begun the conversation. That was out of keeping with the rigid formality usually observed in such situations.

'Not exactly,' he said. 'I sell audio-visual packages. Music produced by the human voice sounds . . . well . . . primitive.'

Cecile's eyes twinkled like stars and again her outline appeared to shimmer.

'If I may say so, Madeas,' she said pleasantly, 'you are singularly ill-informed, even for a Galiterian.'

Madeas felt suddenly embarrassed by his dark green toga with its broad white border, and by his hair, cut and braided in the style of his people. He was not ashamed of the planet that had given him birth, but he was unused to be pigeon-holed in this way by strangers. However, he had been brought up to respect women and so made no reply.

'Singing can very tuneful,' his companion went on. 'If that means it was primitive, so be it. Maybe I prefer the primitive. Nowadays vibrations must be electronically magnified and, of course, there have to be images. The more erotic the better, I'm told.'

'My company, *Transgalactic Inc*, is quite conservative. Nothing too spicy.' Madeas laughed self-consciously. 'And naturally we don't sell the hardware.'

'You don't?'

'No. The Jesydians are much better at micro-circuitry than we are . . . and the Illyans. The Illyans' equipment is reputedly the best.'

Cecile smiled again, showing a set of even teeth. 'So here you are, a Galiterian, bound for Terra at Krismas, with packaged music to sell. The Terrans will like that.' Now her splendid eyes were pregnant with mischief.

'Plenty of vibrations! The tune doesn't matter so long as it shakes the floor. What's the latest thing - olfactory sounds or multidimensional tactile pictures?'

'As I say, my company is rather conservative. We haven't gone that far. Actually, I'm rather sick of the job, and of synchronised imagery and vibrations,' he confided. 'But I have a wife and two children to support. I've been working on a little idea of my own.'

Cecile tilted her chin and looked at him quizzically.

'I might try to market it myself . . . one day. It's an acoustic machine. I call it a chordalin. Would you like to see it?'

'I would like to very much.'

Madeas activated the control in his armrest that would open his locker. He reached for the smaller of two cases that lay inside, placed it on the table between them and released the fastener. He took out an object consisting of a triangular metal frame, about a metre from apex to base, strung horizontally with wires of different lengths.

'What does it do?' Cecile asked.

'It makes music. If it were to take off, it could mean a new musical era. Here, I'll show you.'

Madeas drew on a pair of natural fibre gloves, wedged the apparatus between his knees and began to stroke the strings in a random fashion.

A continuous wave of melodious sound permeated the whole cabin. The low-pitched, almost imperceptible pianissimo on the lower wires was followed by a plaintive mezzoforte on the upper, that hung in the air before building to a powerful crescendo as Madeas struck a final chord in the middle of the instrument.

Watching and listening, Cecile was bombarded with images of scenes long forgotten - of green fields, wispy clouds and gentle breezes rustling the leaves; of ocean winds whipping the sea; of jagged rocks and thunderstorms; of meandering streams and majestic snow-capped mountains.

Madeas had no such visions. He was aware only of the mathematical patterns in his brain and the tingling of his fingers, in their loving partnership with his creation - a symbiosis of organic with the inorganic.

The faint shudder as the shuttle's engines came out of space-drive passed unnoticed.

'That was beautiful,' Cecile gasped. 'Music to make even the Immortal Elders weep.'

'Elders?' Madeas frowned. It wasn't politically correct to mention Religion – or gods or a mystical human self which survived death. There were secret cults, he had heard, but no sane person believed in immortality or spoke about such things. However, despite his rationality, Madeas was delighted by her approval.

'You really liked it? You think it has a future?'

'I'm sure of it, but not on Terra.'

There was a gentle bump as the ship docked. Some of Madeas's enthusiasm died and he looked downcast.

'Whyever not?' he asked, perplexed by the apparent contradiction. 'With their love of music, the Terrans will give me a fair hearing. They have telepathy and I shall have no problem communicating. And you said . . .'

Cecile sighed and shook her head. 'You will never sell the chordalin on Terramagna, more's the pity. Believe me. If I were you I should disembark here on Hermesia.'

Something in her voice convinced Madeas that she meant what she said.

'But I don't understand,' he stammered. 'Why?'

'The second question is the easier to answer.' Everything around her seemed to shimmer in the dimmed cabin lights. Madeas waited.

'There is an old saying,' Cecile said, 'that it's the early bird who catches the worm. Why waste time and parsecs? Market your chordalin here. It will be a success.'

'You know, I believe it will. I suddenly feel a new confidence. Thank you! But about Terra?'

'There is a story . . . it involves the Elders so perhaps you won't believe me . . .'

'I can listen.'

'Terra committed the unforgiveable crime. Some say they polluted the atmosphere, some that they poisoned the seas. Others tell how they killed animals for sport and when species were reduced to a few only, the humans turned on one another. The Elders punished them.

'The Terrans depend for their music on strong vibrations and visual enhancements - effects that can be produced electronically. For them, without strong vibration there is no music. To the Terran, there is no such thing as sound. They could not hear your chordalin even if they wanted to. Every human being on the planet for more than three thousand years has been born without an auditory nerve.'

'As a punishment?'

'So it is said.'

For a moment there was stunned silence. Then Madeas reached for the lighted panel which, at a touch of his forefinger, would send his baggage forward automatically to the customs hall of the planet below.

'I'll take your advice,' he said ruefully, rising and making his way aft.

Cecile remained seated, obviously bound for Illya or even Terraminora and beyond. Once again Madeas noticed the slight shimmering of her figure. It was as if light was able to pass through her body. She was really beautiful, he thought - beautiful and eternal. By all the stars, he was thinking the unthinkable. There was no place for the supernatural in Galiterian society, nor anywhere else in the Universe. Her reference to the Elders had been tasteless. And yet . . .

'I hope to see you again,' he said.

'In time,' she replied, and her voice, though still sensuous in tone, seemed much fainter than before. 'I wish you every success with the chordalin, but I think you should rename it.'

'Rename it? How?'

Her last words were so faint as to be lost amid the noises of disembarkation. It was but a breath of sound that reached him, not by way of molecules vibrating in the ether, but as a voice of inspiration in his own heart.

Cecile closed her eyes as her physical form blended into the ether and out of time. She thought nostalgically of blue skies, ripening corn and the soothing chords of Madeas' new instrument. She had been known by many names – Aoide, who had brought song, Euterpe, who had brought musical delights, even Aphrodite, who had brought love.

It was more than three millennia since she had heard a harp.

ΩΩΩ

Travel

Sashimi, Shoes and Suzuki

Irasshai-mas-ehhhh....!

It is 10.30am in Ginza, Tokyo's fashionable shopping precinct. The Hanyu *depato* has just opened. A dozen assistants assemble on the ground floor to greet the first customers of the day. They form a line. Bow politely. The last syllable of their welcome elongates and fades to the sound of Mozart coming through the loudspeakers. The volume is subdued. Tasteful.

The Imperial Palace is nearby and you are forgiven for thinking the *depato* is being honoured by a royal patron. But no. This quaint ritual is observed every day of the week in every major store throughout Japan. It is a little disconcerting.

Tokyo is vast. Several cities rolled into one. They cater for every taste, from teen fashion to Kabuki theatre and love hotels. Ginza is elegant, Shibuya trendy, Shinjuku brash and crowded. Ueno and Marunouchi offer culture and tranquillity.

Identifying Tokyo's boundary is more a matter of context than geography. As National Capital, it comprises seven prefectures and is home to 40 million people. By UN definitions of urban agglomeration, it has a population of about 28 million. Nearly 8 million live in the *ku* - the inner wards - alone. Its main airport, Narita, is 60 kilometers to the north-east and 60 minutes from Shinjuku railway station.

Now, your destination is Matsumoto, three hours out of Shinjuku to the west. The view gradually changes. Urban agglomeration gives way to middle-class villas with tiny gardens, then to rice fields and small farms. More towns. The train glides into each station and out again within seconds of the scheduled times. Ticket collectors doff their caps and bow as they enter the compartment. On the platform, suited *sararimen* mingle with cute schoolgirls in ultra-short, pleated skirts and rolled-down chunky stockings.

At last you see mountains, distant and snow-capped. The trees still have their autumn colours, but the air is cooler. You enter Nagano Prefecture where Matsumoto nestles in alpine surroundings. Its castle is a national treasure. Begun in 1504 and later remodelled for gun warfare, it has survived the centuries intact.

Matsumoto Castle

When the Americans stay away, westerners are even more conspicuous than usual, especially in the country areas. Small children stare in amazement and nudge their parents excitedly. *Gaikoku-jin desu,* they whisper loudly.

Look, foreigners!

However, you soon forget you are different. After a day or two, bowing becomes second nature. People are friendly. You greet strangers in lifts, restaurants, parks and even in the street in this traditional way. Their responsive *konnichiwa* - hello - is surprised, but spontaneous.

Temple at Nagano-shi

Nagano-shi, the prefecture capital and venue for the 1998 Winter Olympics, is modern metal and glass mixed with touristy shops and shrines. Zenko-ji, one of Japan's finest temples, proclaims welcome to people of all faiths. It lies at the end of a narrow street lined with boutiques peddling lucky charms, enamelled chopsticks and paper dolls. There are restaurants too that hide the delights of Japanese cuisine behind curtained doorways and banks of discarded shoes. The menus in bewildering *kanji* and *hiragana* lend new meaning to the term pot luck.

Back in Matsumoto, you search unsuccessfully for a memorial to one of its most famous sons. Dr Shinichi Suzuki (1898-1998), violin teacher extraordinaire, gave the city its prestigious music academy. However, it seems his life is celebrated more outside Japan. Just one little statue is testimony to his work.

Violinist Statue in Matsumoto

The shops are decorated with Christmas trees and festive bunting. High fashion straight from London, Paris and New York competes with traditional *kimono* and *obi*. Suits are Jaeger and Armani. Ladies' shoes are strapless with fifteen centimeter heels. Apples the size of grapefruit are individually boxed and sell for the price of a modest breakfast. Packaged *sashimi* meals are worth a king's ransom.

Japan is a fascinating land. It is at once mysterious and garish, exotic and commonplace. Racially one of the purest places on earth, it remains one of the least racist in the English sense. High moral ideals coexist with acceptance of public sleaze. Respect for the family is a national virtue, yet Japan is not an equal society. Women dominate the home but men dominate almost everything else.

It is doubtful if Westerners can ever do more than scratch the surface of Japan's history and culture. But through the oriental veil you can catch glimpses of the Japanese character, - their strange indifference to their own heroes, their reluctance to challenge authority or tradition.

It can't be helped, they are fond of saying. *Shiyoo na gai.*

In Kyoto, the *sakura* blossom will be opening, a sure sign that spring has begun. In the Nagano highlands it is still winter.

The mountains that ring Matsumoto stand out, white-capped, in glorious vista-vision against the pale blue sky. In the crisp morning air, they seem closer and more three-dimensional than ever. To the west are the Japanese Alps, soaring to a height of three thousand metres; to the east is a two-thousand-metre-high tableland. A cold wind blows along the valleys of the Susuki and Metoba Rivers. In residential streets, in shady corners where the early April sun does not reach, lie small heaps of snow. It can take a while to melt because, in Nagano Province, each household is responsible for clearing from the roadway adjacent to their property - and Nagano sees a lot of snow.

Matsumoto is not on the main tourist itinerary; however, the city is steeped in history and culture. There is the sixteenth century castle of course, with its amazing collection of weapons, but other museums abound. Possibly the most intrinsically Japanese is the *Ukiyo-e*, the museum of woodblock painting, a style begun in the early sixteen hundreds and for which the country is justly famous. This includes works by Hokusai and Hiroshige, who are known even in the West.

Some attractions are easily found, but the Suzuki School of Music proves elusive. The locals are apologetic, either through apathy or because with your limited Japanese you fail to ask the right question. Fingers point only to lead you astray. Heads are shaken. You suspect that to the natives of Matsumoto the word *Suzuki* conjures up quite a different image to that of the elderly violist with a special understanding of children. At last you find it, not far from the main boulevard, in a back street surrounded by small business premises, the rear walls of department stores and a temple or two. By then the fine morning has given way to cold rain. And the school is closed! The only concert advertised is in Tokyo, three hours away by train.

Shiyoo-na-gai.

Food is never far from your thoughts and, when it comes to meal times, the choice is wide. One option is the packed lunch, or *bento,* purchased in special shops with the slogan 'quick, cheap, tasty.' Quick and tasty they may be, but the better ones are far from cheap. Then there are the sushi parlours, many of which can only be described as 'Americanised'. The small, family-run businesses are more expensive but worth the premium. Making the effort to understand and conform to the customs brings its own reward. Not only is the service exceptional, but a second visit may bring the proprietor to the table with a parting gift.

Better still, drive into the foothills, just beyond the city limits, where lie more exclusive restaurants. There, especially if you are lucky enough to be a guest of a Japanese friend, you can partake of a banquet of traditional fare and enjoy an ambience that only Japan can provide. Squatting is optional. However, the *tatami* is pristine and shoes are public enemy number one. Two pairs of slippers are provided, and woe betide the guest who confuses them. The first is to wear during the meal, the second for visiting the toilet, an unusual pleasure in itself especially if the premises are equipped with the latest Japanese technology - heated loo seats and piped music.

For a different kind of gastronomic experience, visit the *wasabi* farm. *Wasabi* is a kind of horseradish, a very hot, green spice used to flavour *sashimi* and other dishes. It is either grated fresh or made up into a paste for the self-service diners.

In the country that gave us *fugu*, it is perhaps no surprise to learn that *wasabi* has other uses. For a real treat, why not try *wasabi*-flavoured sweets, or something the Japanese call *wasabi-ai-su-ku-ri-mu*. You figure it out!

Sa-yo-na-ra.

The *Shinjuku-eki* in downtown Tokyo is a nightmare.

Imagine Euston, King's Cross and St Pancras all rolled into one, with Piccadilly metro station and Harrods superimposed thereon, and you will have some idea of this uniquely Japanese experience. The guidebooks advise visitors not to panic, but how can you avoid it. Shinjuku is panic with a capital P. It supposedly handles two million passengers a day, and they move through its maze of tiled corridors, lifts and escalators like a video film on fast-forward. Maybe that's the problem for, slow it down and it becomes a haven of logic and master planning. Moreover, it's a gateway to the world. Trains from this station will take you just about anywhere.

The *shinkansen* will whisk you to Kyoto in under two and a half hours. The fare is sixty pounds, and for that you get club class comfort and service. The staff wear gloves and bow on entering and leaving the compartment. In Japan, politeness is everything. The fastest trains reach 300kph and shave about twenty minutes from the journey. At all costs, avoid the temptation to fall asleep in your comfortable armchair unless your destination is also a terminus. Arrival and departure times are finely tuned to the point of suicidal obsession. Ignore this warning and you may wake up in Osaka.

After the sheer hell of Tokyo, Kyoto seems peaceful. (Has anyone ever noticed the anagram?) Its new railway station is a marvel of architecture and design - spacious arrival halls, shopping arcades paved with coloured tile, shiny escalators and twisting stairwells. Its roof is a soaring lattice of metalwork, reminiscent of the Eiffel Tower but more subtle. There is something almost musical about its lines. However, do not be lulled into a false confidence. Despite the multiple information points with English-speaking staff, it is too easy to lose a sense of purpose and direction.

Getting lost is easy. First, count the floors. Kyoto New Station admits to two, labelled plainly 1F and 2F.

What is wrong with that, you ask? Well, 1F is at street level; Japan has followed the custom of the USA and has abolished the ground floor. Moreover, there are not two floors but three or four, if you count the underground system. Find yourself there before you have purchased a map and the following steps no longer matter.

Kyoto Railway Station

Look for somewhere to stow your luggage. There is no shortage of lockers - on the west, on the east, and in the central pedestrian walkway on 2F. Finding one that will accommodate a large suitcase and two bags is quite another matter and when you do, it is invariably taken. However, perseverance pays off; an extensive search along many kilometers of corridor will eventually yield a result.

The next stage is buying lunch. You are spoiled for choice! The Japanese take their eating seriously and, without stepping outside the boundaries of the *eki*, you will find sushi parlours, hamburger joints and cafeterias, as well as a selection of 'proper' restaurants. Alternatively, you can visit the railway company's very own department store, the JR *Isetan*.

Lunch over, it is time to escape from the station and find your hotel. Well, one bank of lockers looks very much like another, even if you have correctly remembered which floor you are on, or which of the many entrances to *Isetan* you used.

After that, Kyoto is easy - with a tiny smattering of the language. German or Russian a problem? You've got to be kidding. Try this one, US tourist style -

Pah-rah-sah-ee-dah hoh-teh-roo mah-deh oh-neh-gah-ee shee-mahs **

Never use an American phrasebook!

From the eleventh floor of the *Isetan* department store in Kyoto station, you can see the whole city. Its rectilinear boulevards of clean, modern buildings - shops, offices and hotels - stretch away into the haze of the hills that surround it on three sides. Criss-crossing them are neat, narrow lanes lined with boutiques and traditional teahouses that speak of an age long gone, when Kyoto was Japan's capital and the *geisha* was queen. Here and there, a temple roof peeps out from a verdant cocoon of maple and pine, while patches of *sakura*, the much-vaunted cherry blossom, make an unlikely appearance midst the jungle of garish neon signs.

To the north and somewhere in the centre of this panorama lies the Imperial Palace, the *Kyoto-gosho*, a complex of buildings set amid stunning gardens, with avenues of acer, cedar and azalea. There are streams crossed by dainty, arched bridges, and well-stocked ornamental ponds. This site was the official residence of the Japanese emperors for five hundred years, though most of the original palace that stood here has long gone, damaged by fire beyond repair. The present buildings were completed only in 1855, just thirteen years before the move to Tokyo. Kyoto had been the capital of Japan for more than a thousand years.

Apart from the palace, the city boasts one castle of note, the early seventeenth century *Nijo-jo*, built by a powerful Shogun, but now public property. It too is set in magnificent gardens. Nijo is a UNESCO World Heritage Site.

Kyoto abounds in gardens, havens of peace and tranquillity in the *Zen* tradition with ancient stones laid in symbolic patterns, arboreta of shapely conifers and mirror pools that teem with enormous carp. Sometimes there are pavilions with walls of paper and wood, their floors laid with *tatami*. There you can squat and, for little more than the price of a downtown coffee, be served with a bowl of green tea and a cake by a *kimono*-clad waitress in a ceremony that is as old as Kyoto itself.

In the evening, the streets are swelling with people, shopping, dining or simply enjoying the spring air by the river. April is the time of the *hanami* - blossom viewing. The Japanese have a thing about the seasons, and they celebrate each in their own special way with ceremonies and festivals, some semi-religious and dignified, others sheer outrageous fun - an excuse for partying, fireworks and plenty of *sake*.

Women in *kimono* and *obi* are still to be seen gliding along in Gion among suited *sararimen* and teenagers with bared midriffs and bright red hair, but real *geisha* are comparatively rare. There are probably no more than two hundred in Kyoto today compared with ten times that number a century ago. They earn their living on the stage or in a semi-secret world the western tourist seldom penetrates. Perhaps it's the secrecy that has led to western misconceptions.

The Golden Temple, Kyoto

These women, more properly called *maiko* and *geiko* - have nothing to do with the sex trade. They are talented entertainers who sing, dance and play musical instruments for the delight of private, exclusive banquets and parties. At their own theatre in Gion, they perform traditional music and dance for the public at large. Their most famous and colourful presentation, the *Miyako Odori*. - the 'Cherry Dances' - is given in April at *hanami* time.

A few of Gion's 'Geisha'

Travelling around Kyoto is relatively simple. There are two main underground lines and, if you can come to terms with the station maze and master the ticket machines, they offer a speedy and comfortable way of traversing the city. The bus service is even more practical - and cheaper - once you pluck up courage to try it. For 220 yen (just over £1 sterling), it will transport you anywhere within the city limits. The main destinations and street names are displayed in *romaji* - English lettering - on an electronic board at the front of the bus, so the language isn't a problem.

Like any city in the world, Kyoto also has its museums, theatres and cinemas. It has fashionable department stores too, but if you are looking for souvenirs, - real souvenirs - visit the smaller shops where specialist advice and personal service are the norm. You might even get a cup of tea. Often there is a price to be paid. Electronic goods - cameras, mobile phones and the like - are inexpensive and funky and you can buy a genuine Japanese fan for around 5,000 yen.

But if you want a kimono, better sell your car first!

[* translation supplied! - "To the Palaceside Hotel, please."]

ΩΩΩ

In the Footsteps of a Queen

Fotheringhay village hides its past well. It comprises a few dwellings, a charming hostelry and a historic church. The River Nene meanders through its fields on the way from the Grand Union Canal at Northampton to the North Sea. From time to time, a narrow boat passes this way and moors by the riverbank. The rural tranquillity, especially on a balmy summer day, is intoxicating.

This tranquillity conceals a history filled with treachery and bloodshed.

Fotheringhay was once a place of some importance. It was here, on February 8th 1587, that Mary Queen of Scots, having been found guilty of complicity in a plot to depose Queen Elizabeth of England, was executed by royal command. All that remains of the great castle where she died are a few stones surrounded by an iron fence, yet today the site attracts visitors from all over the world.

Innocent or guilty, Mary kept her queenly calm to the block itself. She remained true to her Catholic faith despite entreaties by the Dean of Peterborough that she embrace the Protestant religion. Afterwards, her body was preserved at Fotheringhay for six months before being interred in a vault in Peterborough Cathedral. There it remained for twenty-five years until her son, James, who had united the crowns of England and Scotland, transferred it to a tomb in Westminster Abbey.

For a glimpse of Queen Mary's early life, we must travel three hundred miles north, from the Edge of the Fens to the Heart of Midlothian. Mary ruled Scotland for only six years as an adult, from 1561 until 1567, when she abdicated in favour of her son. However, though Holyrood Palace in Edinburgh was Mary's principal home during this time, she was not born there, nor in the city's equally famous castle, but eighteen miles to the west.

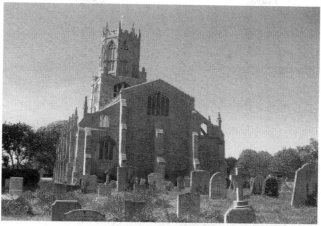

Fotheringhay Church

Mary Stuart was born on December 8th 1542 in the Palace of Linlithgow. She was the only child of King James V of Scotland and Marie de Guise, the daughter of a noble French family. James extended and made considerable improvements to the palace of his ancestors, but he died only a few days after his daughter's birth.

Linlithgow today it is a small county town of twelve thousand inhabitants but in the mid sixteenth century it was, like Fotheringhay, a place of some importance. It lay on the Royal Road linking the castles of Edinburgh and Stirling. In the latter, the nine-month-old baby Mary had the crown of Scotland placed on her head; in the former, as wife of Lord Henry Darnley, she gave birth to the future King James I of Great Britain.

The Palace of Linlithgow still stands. No prince lives there now, but it is still used to stage historic pageants and as a setting for weddings. Even as a ruin, it is a magnificent piece of architecture. Close by and rising above it is the steeple of St Michael's Church, rebuilt in the fifteen hundreds, a century after the fire that destroyed it and much of the town. Both palace and church are worth seeing for their own sakes. They occupy a prime position on a mound overlooking Linlithgow Loch to the north. Just like the village on the banks of the Nene, it is a picturesque spot.

During the first six years of her childhood, Queen Mary knew no fewer than four homes before being shipped to France and eventual marriage with its Dauphin. It was 1561 when she returned to Scotland, and her destiny. She was greeted by cheering Edinburgh crowds. However, her popularity was short-lived. The Scottish lords, Protestant and Catholic alike, vied with each other for her favour. The Calvinists muttered threateningly about her Papist rituals, though it has to be said that Mary did not flaunt her religion in public. Nor did she attempt to undermine the *Kirk*.

In the end, she was brought down not by religion but by love. Mary Stuart fell for and married the handsome but rakish Darnley, son of James V's half-sister. Their only child was born in Edinburgh Castle in 1566.

The room inside the castle's royal apartments where James VI took his first breath is still on the tourist trail today, as are the Crown and Regalia and the St Margaret Chapel, built in the early twelfth century and named after the Saxon princess who was the queen of Malcolm III, successor to Macbeth.

However, it was at Holyrood that one of the most dramatic moments in Mary's life took place - the murder of her favourite, David Rizzio, by Darnley's men. And it was in the nearby house of Kirk o' Field that Darnley himself met his fate on February 9th 1567, murdered, it is widely believed, by the Earl of Bothwell, whom Mary married in May of that same year. She wrote later that their engagement had been *accompanied not the less with force* but of course, there is no independent proof.

Linlithgow Palace with St Michael's Church Steeple in Background

Like most cities, Edinburgh is a mixture of the beautiful and the ugly, the historic and the modern. However, I suppose some of its attraction for me lies in personal association. In a sort of genetic memory, I picture my ancestors as they went about their lives and their business among the teeming thousands - rich and poor, honest and vile - that made Edinburgh what it is today.

One of my great-great-grandfathers, a master builder, walked the streets around Surgeon's Hall and the

University canvassing for work and searching (successfully, I am happy to say) for a young wife. Another was a manufacturer of waterproof clothing for seamen in the port of Leith. A third ran a public house.

All the sights of Edinburgh are worth seeing, but the unmissable delight must surely be the view from the castle ramparts. Perched high on an extinct volcano, Edinburgh Castle stands sentinel over both the old town and the new city. On one side are the dark, narrow wynds where once crept the body-snatchers Burke and Hare, and the respectable but sinister Deacon Brodie, model for Stevenson's Dr Jekyll/Mr Hyde. On the other lie the broad streets, immaculate squares and grand buildings of the eighteenth-century Georgian period. When looking down on Princes Street Gardens, it is difficult to imagine that in their place was once a stinking abomination known as the North Loch, depository for the city's refuse - animal, vegetable and mineral.

Within easy walking distance of the castle esplanade are St Giles Cathedral, the Writers' Museum and the famous Mary King's Close. The house of John Knox, Queen Mary's implacable religious enemy, is not far away. Holyrood, at the other end of the Royal Mile, is a bus or taxi ride for the less athletic.

The story of the so-called Babington Plot that sealed Mary's fate is well documented. It is probable she was a victim rather than a principal conspirator but, of course, this is something we shall never know for sure.

Queen Elizabeth herself was reluctant to condemn her cousin and several historians have suggested even that she was tricked into signing the death warrant. However, this may only be wishful thinking by writers repelled by the barbaric treatment by one queen of another.

As Sir Walter Scott put it, Mary *was, in every sense, one of the most unhappy Princesses that ever lived, from the moment when she came into the world.* She was forty-four when she died, and she had spent nearly twenty of those years in a prison of one sort or another. She had lived for another thirteen in France. She spent only twelve years in her native Scotland, Queen in name yet pawn in a deadly politico-religious chess game. Whatever the truth about her trial and death, it was a tragic end to a tragic life.

ΩΩΩ

Mountain and Flood

As the *Caledonia Isles* steams slowly into Brodick Bay, the peaks of Arran are hidden in a bank of heavy cloud. Thirty years and more roll away in a moment.

It was often like that in the old days, I reflect, the island shrouded in a highland mist that threatened to cast gloom over the most intrepid holidaymaker. It rained. We donned our mackintoshes, sou'westers and wellingtons. We went for walks along muddy tracks and across wet fields, splashing in the puddles and squelching through the sodden grass.

Suddenly, the rain stopped, the mist lifted and the sun came out. The lower hills became visible, the dark green of the forests contrasting vividly with the rich meadowland below. Off came the rainwear. We paddled in the sea. On warmer days, we ventured further out to cool ourselves in the breakers.

Then we could see the mountains in all their grandeur, Goatfell, *Beinn Tarsuinn* and, beyond them, the forbidding crags of *Cir Mhor*.

When I was about two to three years old, my parents rented a cottage at Whiting Bay. It probably still stands, though I have no idea where. I have only a hazy childhood memory of a long low building, painted white, with a sloping expanse of lawn in front. Later, I came to enjoy holidays with them on the island, walking, cycling and climbing, whatever the weather; scrambling over rocks; watching crabs, and tiny fish trapped in rock pools; exploring caves and abandoned shepherds' cottages; listening to Arran's legends. However, it was that view of the mountains from Brodick Bay that stayed firmly in my mind when everything else had begun to fade.

The ferry docks and we wait patiently for the stern door to open. This is not like my last visit in the sixties. Then, I stood on the tilting deck of a small steamer watching the dockers sling the ropes, smelling the seaweed and salt air, listening to the screech of the seagulls as they hovered hopefully above the pierhead. Now, there is only the smell of warm metal and rubber with a hint of diesel and sweat, the sound of slamming doors.

At last we are in the daylight again, clanking over the gangplank to the slipway and up onto the pier tarmac. Somewhere on the island the sun is shining. The clouds that masked Goatfell are being whisked away in the early summer breeze. The age-long fabric of nature is the same: the smooth cone of the mountain framed by a blue sky; the plantations of firs, crowning the hills above Brodick Castle; the sweep of sand along the northern side of the bay.

I wonder how the island has changed in other respects. What happened to the whitewashed cottages on their patchwork of green? Elsewhere, the world has moved on. Modern tourism has destroyed many an idyllic setting. Are the villages of Arran now dominated by four-storey hotels and holiday chalets?

And the people? In our age of violence, crime and prejudice, surely their trusting, open house habits have given way to a more practical, cautious approach to visitors from the outside world. Has their celebrated northern canniness been replaced by a cynical tolerance of the 'townies' who invade their shores?

Unhurried, we drive south out of Brodick. A heavy goods vehicle from the ferry slows to let us pass. There are no skyscrapers and no road rage here! Brexit,

EastEnders and the internet seem a million miles away.

Along leafy lanes, the colour and texture of the foliage changes as the sun bursts through the clouds. Everywhere, the gorse is in full bloom; carpets of wild hyacinths spread through the woods; the gardens are filled brilliant azaleas, pieris and rhododendrons that defy the efforts of gardeners in the Shire Counties.

The sun roof is open and, as we cruise slowly downhill towards Lamlash, the chirped greeting of a family of thrushes is just audible above the purr of the engine.

'Welcome to Arran,' they seem to say. 'Come and go as you please. We never lock our doors here.'

Nothing has changed after all.

ΩΩΩ

Poems and Other Oddities

National Poetry Day

Why must we have poetry
Morning, noon and night?

A media game?

For shame -
Verse to schedule can't be right!

Inspiration is expected.
True Art shall have its way.

Dawn breaks.

The Artist wakes,
Says 'I'll write a poem today!'

Inspiration flows like treacle,
Thick, black and sickly sweet.

Time flies.

The Artist sighs
And gazes at an empty sheet.

'Why does the Muse stay silent?'
Cries he, pale, distraught.

'A word! A breath!
A theme! Love? Death?'

She heeds him not.

'A rhyme!' He cries again 'A theme!
Good or Evil? Joy or Sorrow?'

The Goddess heeds.
She pleads
'Write your poem tomorrow.

'To make today **National Poetry Day**
Your rulers have conspired.

'A game
In Poetry's name -

'And I'm Tired!'

ΩΩΩ

The Millennium Bug

(composed during the last hours of 1999)

Centuries ago, the Prophets of Gloom
Predicted an end of millennium doom.
For reasons which no one could understand,
A dreadful infection would blight the land,
And, though Earth has existed for billions of years,
The world that we knew would collapse round our ears.

'On Hogmanay Night dark clouds will descend,
And civilisation will come to an end.
Before Millennium bells have started to chime,
The sun will have to set for the very last time.
And, on the stroke of midnight, the lights will go out.'
Apocalypse Now! - without any doubt.

'Governments will fall, markets will crash
And every bank in the country will run out of cash;
Cars will break down; trains will derail;
Phones will be dead; computers will fail.
Hospital patients will be certain to die,
And planes will fall right out of the sky.

'Cows will be blighted; milk will go sour;
Food in the freezer go bad on the hour;
Wine become vinegar; cheese turn blue;
And worse still, - our beer will be changed into glue.
And the whole population will turn to drugs
As last-ditch defence 'gainst millennium bugs.'

Yet modern science had no explanation
Why this dread plague should infect every nation.
And holy men were puzzled too
By questions of a different hue.
The End in nineteen-ninety-nine
Was surely just a Christian line?

The Chinese folk had naught to fear -
It was a month or two 'til their New Year.
Nor could Islamic peoples jump the gun -
Their year had three more months to run,
While Jews the world o'er, remember,
Would celebrate theirs in September.

Some clever nerds had placed a bet
That it had something to do with the Internet,
And that when we check our PC dates,
(Supplied by courtesy of Bill Gates)
We'll find that somebody has blundered.
The computers'll think it's nineteen hundred!

This Millennium Bug will go to town;
Communications will come crashing down,
And even billions from our taxes
Won't save our hi-fis, fridges, faxes,
Until, at dawn on New Year's morn,
An epoch of chaos will be born.

And, as noon drew close on the thirty-first,
The folks in Europe still feared the worst.
In Edinburgh, things were under way
For the celebration of Hogmanay,
Or to toast the city's biggest wake

If only for Tradition's sake!
While, in London, Dublin, Paris, Rome,
Most people opted to stay at home.
It was a majority decision,
To watch the End on television.
The BBC had gone Down-Under
To New Zealand.   And no wonder!
For the Prophets' claims were quite specific, -
Armageddon would begin in the South Pacific.

As the clocks struck twelve in the Chatham Isles
The natives' faces wreathed in smiles.
Tongans chanted; Maoris sang;
In Auckland, Brisbane, church bells rang.
Through Sydney, Adelaide and Perth,
Midnight moved across the earth.
In Hong Kong, Beijing, Singapore,
Couples married by the score.
O'er Burma, India, Pakistan,
Oman, Muscat, and Iran;
'Cross Russia, Turkey, Egypt too
The gentle Armageddon flew.

'Til at length, all England knew,
What had been suspected by a few,
That the gloomy forecasters had lied.
It was not at all what had been prophesied.
And the Welsh and Scots and other folks
Saw it was just an enormous hoax.

Then, as dawn broke over the Pacific reef
Governments breathed a sigh of relief.
Markets still stood; the pound suffered no dent;

Even the Euro lost scarcely a cent.
Concorde was zooming again overhead
While all of America was sleeping in bed.
In NHS hospitals, it is such a bore, -
Waiting lists are as long as before.
PC's and the Internet are working just fine.
Our beer is still beer; our wine is still wine.

But 'tis no miracle that we're still alive, -
The Millennium was passed in 'Ninety-five,
For all the experts now agree
That Christ was born in Five BC!

And, if you find these dates confusing,
Terribly trite or vaguely amusing,
Just stop and contemplate. It's clear,
Though life will go on for another year,
That bugs can strike in any season,
In any land, for any reason!

**And remember, the third millennium won't have begun
'Til January First, Two Thousand and One!**

ΩΩΩ

Birthdays

Why do we need birthdays?
Reminders of the passing days,
Labels. Numbers we can never comprehend,
Telling us what our body denies.
Maturity is not arithmetic,
Conveniently measured by the years.
Ageing begins at birth,
But youth lasts as long as we believe:
Old is something for other people.
Why do we need birthdays?

ΩΩΩ

The Magdalene Story

A few miles to the west of Edinburgh, and not far from the Firth of Forth, lies the village of Abercorn. It was a hamlet as early as the seventh century and is mentioned in the annals of the Venerable Bede, the Northumbrian cleric best known for his *History of the English People*.

Today, Abercorn is a mere dot on the map. Indeed, on some maps, it does not appear at all. It comprises a few farms, isolated cottages, an ancient church and very little else. The villages of Newton and Philipstoun to the south are small by any standard. Yet in the 18th Century Abercorn was a parish in its own right and part of the County of Linlithgow. In 1792, it had a population of 870 and stretched from the town of Linlithgow itself in the west to the village of Dalmeny at the southern end of the present day Forth Bridge.

Between Abercorn Church and the shore of the Firth lies Hopetoun House, one of Britain's most beautiful stately homes. Hopetoun is the seat of Adrian Hope, the fourth Marquess of Linlithgow and, until 1987 when he succeeded to that title, the Earl of Hopetoun. Hopetoun House dates from the 17th Century but its later extensions and alterations include some of the best work of the Adam family - William and his sons John, Robert and James. It has often been described as Versailles in miniature. *'The natural beauty of the parish,'* wrote the author of the Statistical Account of the parish in 1799, *'is greatly heightened by the quantity of land which is planted, and the taste with which it has been done.'*

When my story begins in the late 1770s, Abercorn's population was 850. Most adults, both men and women, were employed on the land or in domestic service by owners of the nearby great estates. Wages were not high but employees appear to have been treated well here, even to the extent of support in retirement and widows' benefits. One such estate worker in the employ of the second Earl of Hopetoun was a man called James Spring. He was my four-greats-grandfather.

One of the most recent stones in the churchyard of Abercorn, many of which are much weathered and difficult - if not impossible - to decipher, is a testimony to James's long service. It reads: *James Spring, Forester on the Hopetoun Estate for sixty years, died April 11th 1838 in the 82nd year of his age. His last temporal master caused this stone to be erected as a slight tribute of respect to the memory of a good man and a faithful servant.*

James Spring was born in Banchory on Deeside in 1756. His grandfather seems to have migrated along the River Dee from Aberdeen and settled by the 1720s at a place called Candieshill, near Crathes Castle and its extensive forests. William Spring, James's father, was born there in 1726.

James was about 20 years old when he came to Linlithgowshire to work for the second Earl of Hopetoun. The first mention of him in the estate archives was in February 1780, when he was paid five shillings for a full week's work. That he lived a long life in the Hope family's service is in no way remarkable.

The world of work has changed. The era of big business, corporate lawyers and accountants, multi-tiered health authorities and the five-day week has replaced a simpler age. Then, the grocer or butcher dispensed all the news that mattered, the journeyman was highly respected for his skill, the local doctor and school teacher were admired for their superior knowledge, and men worked from dawn till dusk, six days a week and sometimes more, to provide for their dependants. (Of course, many women worked just as long and hard and some even longer, and unpaid, in the home!)

The James Spring memorial stone in Abercorn churchyard

We may scoff nowadays at cap-doffing and other signs of subservience we read of in 19th Century fiction. The old class system has a lot to answer for; it categorised people according to their birth and accorded them a status in life from which they were rarely, if ever, able to escape. It hindered free expression of social and political views, it hampered reform in education, housing and health, and it sparked revolution all over Europe - though not all revolutions were as bloody as the one in France.

It is undeniable that there were great abuses of power, yet the system was not wholly evil. People had a sense of place; there was little need for pretence because they knew who they were and how they fitted into society at large. Communities thrived on mutual respect, responsibility and loyalty. With enlightened and, moreover, successful employers, life could have been very pleasant, even without modern comforts.

This was the kind of society in which James Spring and his family lived and worked. In return for their loyalty, husbands had a job and a home for life; their continuing welfare and that of their spouses and children concerned the lord of the manor because he, as well as they, benefited from it. Perhaps we should ponder whether the old system has not been replaced by something infinitely worse.

Despite our illusions of freedom, real power is in the hands of wealthy corporations; the hard-won privileges of free education and universal suffrage are scorned by many. In a society dominated by the cult of personality, in which we are free to aspire to anything we like, people laugh at loyalty and respect has largely vanished.

But I digress. By the second half of the 18th Century, one family who were already well established in Abercorn were the Giffords. Robert Gifford and his wife Magdalene Granger had six children, of whom the eldest was Elizabeth, born in the hamlet of Newton in 1762. In those days, the Presbyterian Church took an uncompromising position on pre-marital sex. Let anyone who doubts it study the baptism record of Elizabeth Gifford. Her unfortunate parents were censured for posterity in the following extract: *'Febry. 18th - This day Robert Gifford and Magdalene Granger in Newton had their first Child born in an antenuptual fornication a Daughter and baptised March 4th 1762 Name Elizabeth.'*

In 1781, James Spring was promoted to senior

forester. He moved into a cottage at Parkhead, a tiny hamlet lying between Hopetoun House and Newton village. In 1783 he married, and his bride was Elizabeth, who gave birth to the couple's first child, Magdalene, in December of that year.

The name Magdalene was a popular choice in this part of the country in that era and at the risk of buying into a piece of alternative history I wondered why. There were several *Magdalenes* in the Gifford family tree and would be several more in the generations to follow. The origin of this family name appears to have been in the parish of Kirkliston, which lay the southern border of Abercorn.

Today, the village of Kirkliston is surrounded by modernity - on three sides by motorways and on the fourth by the runway of Edinburgh Airport. However, it once lay on the royal road between Edinburgh and Linlithgow. Magdalene Granger, Elizabeth Gifford's mother, was born there in 1741. *Her* mother's maiden name was Marshall, her grandmother yet another Magdalene. Moreover, there were no fewer than five Magdalene Marshalls born or married in the same period.

There was also *another* Magdalene Granger born in Kirkliston in 1753. Her mother was a Wilkie, and several Magdalene Wilkies had been born in the parish around the turn of the century.

Old records tell us that Kirkliston was once, in the 12th Century, called Temple Liston, and it comprised of estates owned by the Knights Templar. The village church, rebuilt in modern times, was once a Templar church.

Readers of the popular *Da Vinci Code* by Dan Brown, or *The Holy Blood and the Holy Grail* by Baigent, Leigh and Lincoln, will be familiar with the legends: how Mary

Magdalene - she of the Christian Gospels - escaped Palestine to France after the Crucifixion and claim she was the wife of Jesus and carrying his child. Some imaginative writers would go further and state unequivocally that their son would go on to found a dynasty of kings.

Enthusiasts of those works may ponder what circumstances brought the *Magdalene* name to Scotland and consider what its connection might be with the Lothians - and with Leith, which is awash with Templar lore. They may even wish to read the history of the St Clairs of Rosslyn. Yes, they may, but my interest lies elsewhere!

James and Elizabeth Spring had four children altogether - two boys and two girls, although a document inside Abercorn church suggests there were more. After Magdalene came William (1786), James (1789) and finally Margaret (1796). As the family grew, the Springs may have moved into another cottage in the hamlet. It must have been decent accommodation because in 1813 and 1814 a local tax of four and sixpence per annum was levied on it - about 22p of today's money, but a considerable amount in those days. The Parkhead cottages were rebuilt in the late 19th Century and are still occupied today.

By the early eighteen hundreds, James had worked himself up to the position of head forester to the earls. In the years from 1819 to 1822, the Hope family paid him a salary of £35 per annum, and in 1819-1820, he had enough men working for him to run up a wages bill of £380. He also received some payment in kind. Hopetoun was a successful and prosperous estate, and James benefited in other ways, such as receiving very fair expenses for travelling on estate business, which he seems to have done regularly. To celebrate the 1822 visit of King George IV to Hopetoun, he was given six shillings and sixpence that year for the purchase of a new pony bridle!

Natural forest and plantation covered about one sixth of the area of the parish of Abercorn and a major part of it was on Hopetoun land. According to the Statistical Account of 1791, *'Abercorn naturally strikes the eye from the opposite coast of Fife'*. In a later account, the parish minister wrote in glowing terms of Hopetoun's firs and elms, and of its imported species of tree. Those, and *'hard wood trees ... designed as shelter belts for both stock and game'* as well as some field enclosures were included in James Spring's responsibilities.

It is probable that James was still working at the time of his death . There are no records to suggest he was being supported by any of his children. He died on the 11th of April, 1838, leaving a widow, two children and several grandchildren and great-grandchildren. Elizabeth survived him by only nine months.

Magdalene, my three-greats-grandmother, had three sons and two daughters with her husband John Greenfield: Elizabeth, John, James, Agnes and William. The second eldest, John, my great-great-grandfather, born in 1809, became a master builder in Edinburgh. His eldest son, James Spring Greenfield (1851-1890), who was a grocer and wine and spirits merchant in Leith, was my great-grandfather.

There have been no more Magdalenes among my direct ancestors. However there were several in other branches of the family. James's sister, Magdalene Jane (1856-1937) was, according to *her* granddaughter Magdalene (1918-2015), *a lady who loved parties*. James's younger brothers Jack and Alex gave the name to their daughters, Jack going one better and calling his child Magdalene Margaret Spring Greenfield.

My three-greats-grandmother Magdalene Spring Greenfield died at the home of her son William on the 29th October, 1854, a few weeks short of her 71st birthday. She was buried at Newton.

Until now, I have been unable to find her grave.

ΩΩΩ

Feneticks Bee Dammd

A Guide for English Singers Abroad

Nothing matches the excitement of travelling to foreign lands. A change of scene, climate and culture, a bit of sun and sea, or crisp mountain air, are surely all we need to blow away the cobwebs of winter. And nothing compares to the thrill of rising, however imperfectly, to the challenge of a new language.

Why can't they all speak English? I hear you say. Well, it's pretty obvious, isn't it? Just try teaching a Frenchman to say Wellington and Warmington, or a Japanese Leicester and Letchworth and you'll see what I mean. Professor Henry Higgins would have expressed it quite bluntly. Painful to the ears. And I would probably have agreed with him had he not gone on to say that he'd rather hear a choir singing flat. Poor Henry Higgins! He was right about so many things but about singing, No. A thousand times No! Better five hundred Frenchmen and five hundred Japanese ...

Which brings me back to my theme. We singers would of course like to make a good impression on our foreign cousins - pure tones, perfectly balanced harmonies, clear diction - and if we can make them sit up and take notice with some well-rehearsed numbers in their own tongue so much the better. But where do we begin? It's bad enough having to learn the music without having to pronounce those foreign words as well.

Did someone mention phonetics? We can't even agree on our own language, for goodness sake. *Ough!* Is it *ow, uff, off* or *o*? What about those *a*'s - do we take a *chawnce*, or would we rather *dunce*? Should we always aspirate, or do we concede, like Henry again, that *in otfid, erifid and empsha urrikines odly hevva epin?*

Langenscheidt's Dictionary, that bastion of the German language, gives the following instructions for the pronunciation of the English *w* - very short *u* - not a German *w*, and it urges the would-be enunciator of the diphthong *th* to adopt a lisp.

And for *r* - do not roll! Not very illuminating for anyone aspiring to the poetry of Mozart's *Zauberflöte*, but it does give some idea what we're up against, in reverse.

It wouldn't be so bad if all Germans, say, spoke the same way, but they're like us, you see. From Munich to Berlin or Hamburg is about as far as London to Dublin or Edinburgh, and the differences are about as confusing. Should we make that final *g* into a *k* or squelch it like the Scotsman's *loch*? Does the *r* roll forward on the tip of the tongue or disappear down the back of the throat? Must we differentiate between *s* and *z*?

Or perhaps we should, after all, just admit defeat. Like true disciples of the Professor, accept his axion that one common language I'm afraid we'll never get.

Go with the flow!

ΩΩΩ

A Bat's Ear View

I sometimes think summer evenings are worst.

Though a girl feels like a bit of exercise after hanging around all day, it just isn't possible in this weather. I know our front door's in the shade of the trees, and when it's overcast the family can look forward to a flutter among the tombstones before dinner, but this sunshine is the pits. Drack is always so laid back about it all. Says I should chill out, whatever that means.

There's going to be another concert in the church. I was just dropping off to sleep last Sunday morning after a difficult night with the kids when I heard them talking down in the porch, the vicar and the warden. A choir apparently. I don't think they've been here before. There's to be an instrumentalist too, a cellist - now there's something we don't hear every night of the week - oh, and a bunch of children! Bram, our youngest, has been off his food for a few days, so I'm hoping the music isn't going to upset him.

No, sweetheart, you can't go out to play!

Sorry, that was Mina, one of the twins. What was I saying? Oh yes, a concert. It's really is a pity they've done such a good job patching up the holes in the church roof. We used to get down quite a lot, you know, have a proper look as well as a listen.

I know what you're thinking, and it isn't true. From up there in the eaves everything down there looks a bit fuzzy, but blind we are not! I don't know how that rumour got about. Just because the big folk have only five senses -

There are quite a lot of the locals in the church already and more are arriving. I can hear car doors slamming down the high street, so that must be the visitors and their travelling fans.

Two feet, Mina! Yes, I know you can fly, but mummy knows best.

Honestly, I think we're raising a rebel there. She can be very stubborn. Why are they applauding? The concert hasn't even started.

Go back to sleep, Vlad. Daddy'll be home soon.

Where was I? Oh yes, the choir. The acoustics in here are pretty good, so I hope they'll keep the volume down, especially those high voices. We had a different choir a few months ago and the sopranos were murder. It's OK for these humans with their auditory nerves tuned to lower frequencies, but we nocturnals are different.

Actually, this lot aren't bad. Nice balance. If anything, a bit towards the bass register. Cool. What's that they're singing? I'm not much good at human language, but it sounds like they're telling me to go to sleep. I wish! Shut-eye is a luxury when you have four kids. Do these singers know nothing about our species? They even have an expression for us. *Blind as a . . .* Well, you know.

I don't understand this one at all. What sort of language is that? Foreign; Welsh or Irish maybe.

Ah, this one's better. Good tune and words I can understand. I haven't heard it before but by the Impaler's blood, why do they have to sing it all *fortissimo*. And something's not quite right there. That fellow, third from the right I think, basses they call them. Yes, my friend, you were just a teeny-weeny bit flat on that lower note, about an eighth of a semitone. And the lady in the middle of the front row . . . That was a glissando if ever I heard one. I'll do a few circuits of the nave. Perhaps if they know I'm here they'll tone it down.

The audience is clapping again. Have they

finished? Lots of chatter. The clink of glasses. I thought it was too good to be true.   Lord, what are they doing now? Moving the furniture? Kinky.

The air currents are back. Seems we're to have more music. Just a quick buzz round while they warm up. I've got cramp in this left wing.

No, Bram, you can't have a drink. It isn't polite to bite the visitors.

Now it's the turn of the children. Now that was a jolly song. I could get used to this singing. But now the big folk are back, and not quite as tuneful as before. I'm guessing a few got tanked up on wine at the interval. An' that was a *real* Scots accent. What about the man who's speaking? I wonder why they laughed. I wish I'd taken human humour as an option at Cambridge.

Go to sleep at once, Vlad. I won't tell you again. No! No story. Not even 'Buffy and the Buckets of Blood'. Maybe daddy'll read it to you tomorrow.

ΩΩΩ

In My Own Write

THANK YOU FOR READING *IN MY OWN WRITE*!
PLEASE READ ON FOR AN EXTRACT FROM *IT'S A
FANTASY WORLD!*

It's a Fantasy World!
Exploring the Best Fantasy of Page and Screen

1: Dreaming the Impossible

We live in a universe of wonders and possibilities.

The ancients looked up into the night sky and saw bright lights formed into the shapes of fish, dogs, human figures and other familiar objects. When they reached out to touch the lights, they may have been surprised to discover they could not. They may have imagined the Sun and Moon as powerful gods, pursuing one another through the heavens as night changed to day and day to night. When the hunt was unsuccessful or a harvest failed, they may have blamed these beings. Perhaps they sought to pacify them with gifts or sacrifices. When nature brought bounty or new life, these primitive humans would pile more gifts on their altars with prayers that their good fortune might continue.

The everyday winds, tides, springs and sounds of nature they may have supposed to be under the control of lesser spirits. When their nights were overcast and there was no starlight, they no doubt imagined monsters and demons and told tales to warn their children of dangers lurking in the darkness. Generations of shamans and priests would play on fears of the unknown to exercise control over the tribes, because fear in one group meant power for another.

Today, most of us scorn and laugh at such ideas. When we look up, we see other suns, and galaxies, and pulsars, and we try to imagine fourteen billion years of cosmic expansion. We speculate about what caused the first spark that started it all, and about how the universe will end.

Humans have invented and built machines that travel faster than sound. We have space vehicles that can escape Earth's gravity and travel to the limits of our solar system and beyond - that can even send back pictures and data that tell us what the distant planets look like and how they are composed. We can send packages of information at the speed of light using other machines no bigger than the palm of a human hand, and with the same devices receive messages and pictures from the other side of the world. Such devices make use of laws that scientists call quantum mechanics but which no one, not even the scientist, seems to fully understand.

We know that the Moon controls the tides; that winds are caused by variations in atmospheric pressure and earthquakes by movement in tectonic plates. We know all these things but there is still so much we do not know about this planet we live on and about the universe around us. We can move information at the speed of light but have not yet learned how to move anything else as fast. We can look into the vastness of space and the minuscule world of the photon and quark but we do not yet know or understand the mathematical and physical laws which connect the very large with the very small.

And we laugh at the primitive superstitions and rituals of the ancients. We call them fantasy.

The ancients might have used the same word to describe our world. Perhaps they would call our aeroplanes, our mobile phones, our computers and our instant messages 'magic'. A man or woman of 1800 would have put the same label on the scientific achievements of the last fifty years, or at very least called them 'impossible'. Even now, as we stare out into that fourteen-billion-year void, we look beyond the horizon of the possible and achievable into fantasies of our own.

Are we alone in the universe, a single intelligence among the quadrillions or quintillions of other star systems out there? And if not, will we ever find a way of communicating with the others, and of reaching them? Are wormholes real? Is time reversible?

These are some of the fantasies of today - the realms of the impossible - just as, for our ancestors, flying, X-rays, solar heating and television would have been magic in their age. And we wonder, as they wondered. We dream, as they dreamed.

And these dreams we translate into stories, on the pages of a book, an electronic reader or a movie screen. Our fantasies are all around. Perhaps one day . . .

We live in a world of wonders . . . and possibilities.

Printed in Poland
by Amazon Fulfillment
Poland Sp. z o.o., Wrocław

61986838R00047